If Only I Had

*A story for Serenity
from her grandma*

www.mascotbooks.com

If Only I Had

Mascot Books
560 Herndon Parkway #120
Herndon, VA 20170
info@mascotbooks.com

PBANG1116A

Library of Congress Control Number: 2016911644
ISBN-13: 9781631777745

Printed in the United States

If Only I Had

Gillian Hughes

Illustrated By
Anne Bergstrom

Granny

The girl lived with her granny in an old white house near a meadow. Some of the shingles had fallen off the roof, and the front porch was rickety and needed a coat of paint, but it was a good house. She had no brothers or sisters to play with, but Granny was good company. They sometimes played Candy Land and Sorry, or Go Fish, and they often made pretty picture puzzles. But the best part of each day was when Granny reached up to the high shelf and pulled down a book. When she was sitting comfortably in her old rocking chair, she would pat her knee and beckon to the girl.

"Come, child," she would say.

The girl loved to sit curled up in Granny's lap. She couldn't read the words in the book yet, but she looked at the pictures and imagined that she belonged in the stories that Granny read to her. She would be the beautiful princess, or one of Santa's elves, or part of the group of kids at the zoo, laughing at the monkeys or staring with awe at the big brown bears—all of the things she didn't get to do in her small world. Come rain or shine, no matter what, they had story time every night after supper.

Baking day was always fun. Chocolate chip cookies were the girl's favorite thing to make, and sometimes Granny would let her help knead the dough for the big, fat loaves of bread that she baked in the old black oven.

There was always work to be done to keep them busy. Granny had even shown her how to knit and how to sew a button on her dress.

Then there were the chickens to be fed. The girl liked to feed the chickens because she got to use the big yellow scoop to measure out the grain from the barrel where Granny stored it. She could throw the grain all over the yard and make a big mess, but the hungry chickens would eat it all up, so Granny wouldn't get cross. The chickens laid lots of eggs—too many for the girl and Granny to eat—so they rode on the bus once a week to sell the eggs at the market in the small town near where they lived.

The girl needed to get to bed early because Market Day was the next day. She kissed Granny goodnight, then climbed the stairs to her small room and was soon fast asleep.

The sun was just rising above the trees at the edge of the meadow and the birds outside her window were making a very noisy start to their day. The girl was just waking when she heard the knock on her door: "Time to get up child, today is Market Day!" Granny called out.

She dressed herself in a clean but faded blue dress, washed her face and hands, and brushed her teeth, then rushed down the stairs to where Granny was waiting with her breakfast.

As they reached the bus stop, the girl started to get excited. *I wonder if I shall see anything new today*, she thought.

With a sigh of relief, Granny placed the basket of eggs on the ground beside her. "I'm sure these eggs get heavier every day."

"Maybe our chickens lay bigger eggs on purpose," the girl giggled.

With that, the big red bus came lumbering up the road, the brakes wheezing as it pulled to a stop. Granny lifted the basket and slowly climbed the steps onto the bus. The girl followed. The driver closed the door, got in his seat, and off they went.

Not many cars came that way, so the road was quite rough and bumpy. The girl was enjoying getting bounced up and down in her seat, but Granny was not too pleased. Finally, the driver brought them to where the market was being held, and the bus came to a halt.

The girl loved to go to the market. She liked to watch all of the people jostling about, and she liked to touch the fruits and vegetables—to feel the rough husks of the corn and the soft furry peaches, which were displayed under brightly colored awnings. Best of all, she loved how it smelled. Ah, such delicious smells: apples and oranges, radishes and cucumbers, and best of all, the popcorn that the popcorn vendor sold.

Granny will buy me popcorn before we leave

the market. *She always buys me popcorn to eat while we ride home on the bus,* she thought to herself. In the meantime, Granny was busy setting up a place to sell her eggs, so the girl asked if she needed help.

"No, thank you," Granny replied. "You may look around, but don't wander too far."

First, the girl checked to see if the fruits and vegetables stand was open yet. She saw the bright orange awning, with the man who sold his farm produce standing big and tall behind his counter. As always, he was wearing his long, black-and-white striped apron, and a white ball cap on his bald head.

"Hello, Mister! I was just looking to see if you were here today." Waving goodbye, she went on her way—and there it was!

The Hat

A hat! It has to be a hat, with all those flowers and ribbons tied around the brim. But no one was under it, and it appeared to be sliding across a cloth-covered table all by itself.

As the girl looked, mystified at this strange spectacle, she heard a voice.

"Won't be a minute, just sorting out my hats." With that, up popped a very lovely lady. She wore a big smile on her face, and the hat was perched jauntily on her head. Mystery solved!

"Can I help you find something? I have hats for all occasions." The lady smiled kindly at the girl.

The girl shook her head, knowing that it would probably cost too much for Granny to pay.

"No," she answered politely, "I'd just like to look, if you don't mind."

Granny will be pleased that I remembered my manners, she thought.

The lady told her, "You may come inside, but be careful. Some of the flowers are very fragile."

The girl didn't know what that word meant, but decided she'd better keep her hands to herself around anything with flowers.

The lovely lady let her wander around to look at the many hats. Some were hanging from hooks, and others were displayed on bright pink shelves. There were felt ones and straw ones and some made of cloth; hats adorned with flowers and even imitation fruit, and ribbons of every color.

The girl picked up a small straw hat. She liked the yellow ribbons that wound around the brim and hung down the back. "May I please try this on?"

"Oh, this hat was made just for you! Please try it on!" the lovely lady exclaimed, placing it right on the girl's head. "You must have this hat."

The girl shook her head sadly and removed the hat. "It will cost too much for my granny to pay."

As she turned to leave, the lady called out to stop her. "Ask your granny if she will give me two of her best brown eggs. If she says yes, come back with the eggs and the hat is yours."

The girl was thrilled, and so she rushed back to where Granny was just closing down her stand.

"Oh, Granny, have you sold all of the eggs?" she cried.

Granny looked up in surprise. "Well no, child, I still have two of the brown ones left."

The girl told her about the hat with the yellow ribbons.

After making sure that they had left everything clean and tidy, and with Granny carefully carrying the last two brown eggs,

they went in search of the lady at the hat shop. They were lucky to find her still there.

"Business is slow today, I was just about to close," she said as the girl approached with her granny. "Ah, you brought me the two brown eggs! Enjoy the hat."

She put the hat on the little girl's head and began wrapping the eggs in crisp white paper. She placed the eggs in her pocket. "I must be off!" The lady smiled again, and amidst a flurry of skirts and ribbons, she was gone.

Relieved, Granny turned to the little girl. "Next stop is the popcorn vendor, and then home."

They boarded the bus carrying more than they had come with. They only rode on the bus to town on Market Day, so it was a good time to buy the things they needed.

Granny sat down on the bus seat with a loud sigh. "It's good to get off my feet, child," she declared.

But the girl hardly heard her. She was busy munching on her popcorn and day-dreaming about all she had seen and done on Market Day. Granny dozed in her seat, not even grumbling about the bumpy ride home.

It's been another wonderful day, and my granny takes good care of me and loves me a whole lot, but sometimes I feel so sad.

"If only I had…" she whispered to herself.

The Shoes

The next day arrived warm and sunny. The birds outside were making their usual ruckus, and the girl awoke from a dream about black-and-white striped aprons, and popcorn, and beautifully trimmed hats.

Rubbing the sleep from her eyes, she trudged slowly down the stairs. She wondered if Granny was up yet.

Granny looked up from where she sat at

the table, sipping her morning tea. "Of course I'm up, child. But I'm a little tired after our busy day yesterday, so we're going to have a Do-Nothing Day today."

The girl didn't like Do-Nothing Days— they were boring. *I could play with my dollhouse that Grampa made for me before he went away, I suppose, or color in my new coloring book. But those are things to do on rainy days*, she decided, so she asked Granny, "Can I go outside after breakfast and play in the meadow?"

"Yes," Granny answered. "But remember, I can only see you from the window while you're in the meadow. You are not to go beyond the trees."

The girl wandered across the meadow. The soft new grass felt good under her bare feet. She looked around as she went. *It is very quiet out here all by myself. Perhaps this is not such a good idea after all.*

She sat on an old, scarred tree log near the edge of the meadow. She felt so sad and lonely as she looked around. It was a beautiful spring day—the trees were growing new leaves and the grass was changing from brown to green, but she saw just a vast and empty space.

If only I had... she thought.

All at once there was the sound of birds in the nearby trees; a hustling and bustling, as if they were about to begin their day with something special. And then it started: first a high trill from one of the birds as if gathering all of its friends together, and then the most glorious singing, more perfect than anything ever heard before. But the girl hardly noticed.

Once the birds were settled back into their homes among the trees, they saw that the girl hadn't moved from her place on the log. She sat very still, looking just as sad as ever.

If only I had… she thought.

One of the birds, a beautiful black bird with yellow tips on her wings, wondered what could make this girl so sad on such a lovely spring morning, so she flew down to get a closer look. That was when she noticed that the poor child had no shoes. *Oh, dear me,* the bird thought. *Surely if she had some shoes she would be happy.*

The bird with the yellow-tipped wings flew back up into the trees to tell her friends what she had discovered.

"What shall we do?" she chirped.

"What shall we do, what shall we do?" all of her friends chorused.

A wise old owl perched up high in an old oak tree was watching all of the commotion in his superior fashion. He *whoo-whoo*ed, "Why, you make her some shoes, of course!"

This started a chirping and twittering among the birds so loud that the bird with the yellow-tipped wings had to whistle to make them quiet down.

"What do we use?" she trilled, and her friends chorused in response, "What do we use, what do we use?"

"We use what we see," she declared.

The other birds fluttered in agreement. "So, what do we see, what do we see?"

Then an older, more sensible bird pointed out, "Why, the trees, of course!"

While the older birds gathered together to figure out how to make a pair of shoes, all of the younger birds were sent off to gather the materials needed. When the young ones returned, they brought with them leaves of all shapes and sizes, pine needles, small twigs, and pieces of the soft lining from their nests.

The older birds approved of everything the young ones had foraged except for the pine needles, which they discarded, because they were sharp and they might poke at the girl's small toes. Everyone was pleased and sure that they could make a fine pair of shoes.

First, they set the leaves on the ground to sort them out into shapes and sizes. Because it was spring and they were all soft new leaves, the birds decided to weave them together.

It took many days to complete the task, but when it was done the birds had crafted a beautiful pair of shoes.

"Oh my," chirped the bird with the yellow-tipped wings. "What a splendid pair of shoes! But they need one more thing. We must make them soft inside, like we do for our very own nests."

Using the soft lining that the young birds had taken from their nests, it took many more days for the birds to complete the task. When it was done, the birds gathered around to admire their work.

"Oh my," declared the bird with the yellow-tipped wings. "What a super-splendid pair of shoes! But they just need one more thing. We must make buckles for these magnificent shoes."

So, using the twigs gathered by the young birds, the older birds wove the twigs together until they formed two bright, shiny buckles.

"Oh my!" exclaimed the bird with the yellow-tipped wings. "We have succeeded beyond anything I could have imagined. We have made the most super-splendid, magnificent shoes ever! Now all we have to do is give them to the girl."

New Friends

In all that time, the girl had not come back to the meadow to sit on the log.

From a distance, the birds had seen her as she helped her granny hang out the washing. They had heard her laughter when she would run between the clothes on the line as they moved in the breeze. On Market Day they had watched the girl walk slowly to the bus stop. But not once had she ventured toward the log by the meadow.

It was almost summer when she finally came again.

As she bent to wipe the dirt off the log before sitting down, she noticed a little hollow in the log. Inside it, she found the shiny new shoes.

I wonder who they belong to, she thought. And having no shoes of her own, she decided, *Maybe I could try them on.*

They were so comfortable, and fit just perfectly, so she decided to keep them on, just for a little while.

Suddenly, the air was filled with song. The birds were so happy that the girl had returned and found the shoes. Now all they had to do was let her know that they were hers.

"How do we tell her they are for her? How do we tell her, how do we tell her?" they sang.

Then, as if she understood their song, she smiled up at them, filled with gratitude. "Thank you, birds."

She lingered on the log for a very long time, still feeling sad and alone.

If only I had… she thought.

Then they arrived: not one or two, but a whole tribe of rabbits, chasing and nudging each other playfully. *What that girl needs is a friend,* they decided, so they twitched their noses, thumped their feet, and wiggled their short, fluffy tails, trying to get her attention.

When she finally noticed them, she watched their antics for a while, then happily joined them in their play. The rabbits and the girl raced around in the meadow and in and out of the trees, some hiding behind bushes and waiting to be found. The rabbits were excellent at leapfrog and other jumping games, and soon had the girl laughing at their antics.

Her granny watched from the window of the old white house. "Ah, the child has found some little friends to play with," she sighed contentedly as she went back to her ironing.

After a while, both the girl and the rabbits were so tired that they needed to rest, so they sat in a circle on the soft grass. There were flowers growing around her that the girl had never noticed before. She knew that the white ones with the yellow centers were called "daisies," and the bright yellow ones shaped like little teacups were called "buttercups."

"We can do some fun things with flowers,"

*coo-coo*ed one of the rabbits. "Let me show you."

She plucked a buttercup from beside her and held it under the girl's chin. "Your chin has turned yellow," she giggled.

Another rabbit hopped up to the girl with a big bunch of daisies that she had gathered from the meadow.

"We sometimes make daisy chains," she cooed. She showed the girl how to make a small hole in the stalk of one daisy, and then thread the next daisy through the hole. Working together, they made lots of daisy chains.

"What do we do with them now?" the girl asked. "Why, we wear them, of course. On our heads, around our necks, and even around our feet sometimes!" they chorused.

The day had cooled and the sun was going

down. It was almost time for the rabbits to return to their burrows and for the girl to leave the meadow.

A very shy rabbit, who had been watching from the edge of the circle, handed the girl a bouquet of the most beautiful flowers she had ever seen. They were daintily colored in pinks, blues, and purples.

Wearing a daisy chain in her hair and clutching the flowers in her small hand, the girl decided to sit back down on the log for a little while. She was so pleased with her new shoes, and she had made many new friends, but she thought once again, *If only I had…*

Squirrels Get Busy

The summer days were long and warm, and the girl came often to sit on the log by the meadow. She looked each day for the rabbits, hoping they might come to play again, but she supposed they must have found some new place to have their fun. This made her feel sad and lonely all over again, and she thought, *If only I had…*

One day, as she sat there, she felt something

nudge her knee. A fat-cheeked squirrel stared up at her, wondering why she looked so sad.

The squirrel bounded off to find her friends and tell them about the girl who was sitting on the log looking so unhappy.

"I think she needs a friend," squeaked the fat-cheeked squirrel.

"No," chattered another squirrel. "The rabbits already tried that. It made her happy for a little while, but later she was still sad."

Then one of the more curious young squirrels ventured closer to the girl to get a better look. The young squirrel noticed that the girl was wearing the beautiful new shoes that the birds had made for her, but he also saw that she wore a faded and worn dress. The young squirrel rushed back to join his friends.

"I know what she needs," he chattered.

"What does she need, what does she need?" chorused the other squirrels.

In a know-it-all tone, the young squirrel told them, "Her dress is faded and worn. Why don't we get her a new dress?"

The squirrels gathered around in a circle and murmured among themselves. "That's all very fine, but how do we find her a dress?" they wondered.

The wise old owl, who was still perched up high in the old oak tree, was once again watching all of the commotion. In his superior fashion he *whoo-whoo*ed, "Why, you make her a dress, of course!"

Now the squirrels were really confused. "How do we make a dress? But how do we make a dress?" they wondered.

"We use what we see," said an older, more sensible squirrel.

He was met with a chorus of, "So, what do we see, what do we see?"

The older, more sensible squirrel chittered, "Why, the things around us, of course!"

Now that the days were getting shorter and darkness would soon be upon them, the squirrels decided to wait until the next morning to begin searching for the things they would need to make the girl a new dress.

Bright and early the next day, when the dew was still shining on the grass in the meadow, the squirrels went to work looking for something suitable for a new dress. Then a young squirrel saw that the sun was shining on the cobwebs in the bushes, which were still covered with morning dew. The cobwebs shone like silver threads.

"I found it, I found it!" he hollered, stomping his feet.

"What did you find, what did you find?" the other squirrels chorused. And then they saw what the young squirrel was looking at.

"Oh, what a glorious sight!" declared the older, more sensible squirrel. "I know a friend who can spin these webs into the most beautiful dress. All of you must get to work and gather as many of the cobwebs as you can, before the sun dries the dew from them."

A very old squirrel, whose job it was to fix things, bent soft sticks into hoops for the young ones to use to scoop up the webs. It made the job quicker, but it still took many days for them to gather enough dew-laden cobwebs, and many more days for the sensible squirrel's friend to spin the webs into a beautiful dress.

"Oh my," said the squirrel with the fat cheeks. "What a splendid dress! But it needs one more thing. It would be prettier if it had some buttons."

So the older, more sensible squirrel sent the others off to search for buttons.

It didn't take the squirrels long to find what they were looking for. Because fall was near, there were plenty of berries on the bushes and trees, so they had lots to choose from.

The old squirrel who had spun the dress asked, "Which do I use?"

"Which does she use, which does she use?" the squirrels chorused in response.

The old squirrel chose the red holly berries for buttons. "I think the red holly berries will brighten up the girl's day."

When it was done, the squirrels gathered around to admire their work.

"What a super splendid dress this is!"

"Oh my," gasped the squirrel with the fat cheeks. "What a super-splendid dress! But it just needs one more thing. We must make a ribbon for her hair to match the dress."

So, using the rest of the cobwebs that the old squirrel had saved, she spun a magnificent hair ribbon. Then she squeezed the juice from some leftover holly berries and colored the hair ribbon a bright red to match the buttons on the dress.

"Oh my." The fat-cheeked squirrel hopped with excitement. "We have succeeded beyond anything we could have imagined! We have made the most super-splendid, magnificent dress and matching hair ribbon ever. Now all we have to do is give it to the girl."

The Dress

The weather was cooling and the days were getting shorter. It had been a long time since the girl had come to sit on the old tree log. The once-green leaves on the trees had turned into the most glorious shades of red, yellow, and gold. Soon they would dry up and fall to the ground.

The creatures who lived in the meadow and surrounding trees were busy preparing for the coming winter. Some of the birds had flown away to spend time in warmer places. The rabbits were busy making sure that their burrows would keep them warm when the frost and snow came to the meadow. The squirrels were busy gathering enough acorns from beneath the old oak tree where the wise old owl lived. The acorns would keep the squirrels fed when it was too wet and cold outside to leave their homes.

Many days had gone by, and the girl still hadn't come again to sit on the log near the meadow.

"Maybe she moved away," the birds twittered.

"Oh no, she didn't move away—see where

the smoke curls up from the chimney of the house where she lives?" The wise old owl pointed to the old white house.

"Maybe she doesn't like us anymore," the rabbits suggested.

"Maybe if we wish hard enough, she will be here tomorrow," chattered the squirrels.

The next morning dawned cold and damp. Big dark clouds covered the sun, and the smell of coming rain hung in the air.

It began to rain, and the rain lasted for three whole days. The creatures who lived in the meadow and nearby trees left their homes only to forage for food or to check on their neighbors.

During the time the girl was confined to the house, she and Granny filled their time playing board games and a new game called "I Spy with My Little Eye." They made cookies and bread and the girl helped Granny fix supper each evening.

Despite the rain, Market Day was coming up the next day and the girl asked, "Will we be going to the market tomorrow, Granny?"

"I don't think so child, this heavy rain isn't going to let up any time soon. There won't be enough customers for us to make it worth the trip."

The girl was disappointed but she couldn't blame her granny for the rain so she wandered off to play with her doll house. That evening after supper she went to sit on Granny's lap for her nightly story. As her granny started to reach for a book the girl said, "Tell me a story out of your head please, Granny, I love the stories you make up."

So her granny began, "This is a story about a little girl who wanted to be a dancer. Once upon a time there was a little girl named Susie..."

As her granny tucked her into bed the girl said, "I love you, Granny, that was the best story ever."

On the fourth day, the sky was finally bright and clear, except for the occasional fluffy white cloud floating by. The few birds that hadn't yet flown to warmer places before winter were twittering and singing to welcome the new day. Rabbits and squirrels ran and jumped in the meadow, enjoying their freedom after being cooped up for such a long time.

The older squirrels were watching their young ones play.

I wonder if the girl will come today, the fat-cheeked squirrel thought.

I hope the girl comes today, wished the old squirrel who had spun the dress.

Then suddenly, there she was, walking slowly toward the old log near the meadow.

The girl looked around. She saw the birds high up in the trees, and heard them singing their morning song. She saw the rabbits and squirrels playing in the meadow, and noticed the older animals watching their young ones at play.

If only I had… she thought.

As she approached the familiar place where

she often sat, the girl could see something shiny poking out of the hollow in the log.

This is where I found the shoes that the birds made for me, she thought to herself. *Maybe there's something else in there just for me.*

As she got closer, she could see that the shiny thing poking out of the hollow was some kind of cloth object. Gently, she tugged and pulled until the thing came free. Holding it up against her chest she discovered it was a dress—the finest, softest, most beautifully spun dress ever.

Knowing, as if by magic, that the garment was made just for her, the girl slipped it on over her old, faded dress. It fit just perfectly. She was filled with joy as she fastened the shiny red buttons that marched all the way up from her waist to her neck. Then, as she

looked down at the new shoes that the birds had made for her, she saw something else: a bright red ribbon for her hair.

The girl was so busy that she didn't notice the squirrels coming into the meadow. They crept closer and closer until they were almost at her feet. As she tied the ribbon into her hair, she saw them jumping up and down around her, all looking very pleased with themselves.

"Thank you! Thank you squirrels, for the beautiful dress and the ribbon for my hair!" The girl was thrilled. She danced and spun around so that the dress sparkled in the sunlight and the soft silver cloth floated about her legs.

The squirrels were very pleased that the dress was such a success. Then, one by one, they all gradually wandered off to do other things while the girl sat on the log, day-dreaming.

She knew how lucky she was. The birds had made her the most beautiful pair of new shoes because her feet were bare. The rabbits had come to play with her, so she was no longer lonely. The squirrels saw that her dress was old and worn, so they had made her a lovely new one, with a hair ribbon to match. *So why, oh why, am I so sad?* she still wondered to herself. But she already knew the answer.

If only I had... she thought.

The Coat

And then they came, walking cautiously out of the trees: a whole family of deer, led by a majestic old stag. His magnificent antlers stood around his head like a royal crown.

The girl didn't notice them as they wandered into the meadow, digging with their hooves for roots and chomping at the grass as they went.

Then a doe with soft brown eyes saw her.

Wanting to get a better look, the deer edged closer and closer to the girl. *Even though the girl is wearing comfy new shoes, and she's wearing such a beautiful dress, with a ribbon in her hair, how sad she seems!* thought the doe.

A cool breeze cut through the meadow, and the girl stirred from her daydreams. She started to shiver and rubbed her bare arms. *It's getting cold. I should leave the meadow now,* she thought. Then she saw the family of deer who were watching her with interest. *How happy they look.* She rose from the log and headed on her way back to the old white house.

If only I had… she wished once again.

The doe with the soft brown eyes gathered her family together to tell them about the girl who seemed so sad.

"She was shivering when the breeze came

through the meadow," the doe grunted softly. "I think what she needs is a warm winter coat."

The stag pawed the ground. "Girls don't grow thick fur to keep them warm in the winter like we do, so we must get her a coat."

That sounds like a good idea, the family of deer decided as they murmured among themselves. "But how do we find her a coat?"

The wise old owl, who was still perched high in the old oak tree, watched and listened to this latest problem facing the animals and birds that lived near the meadow. He thought to himself, *I suppose I'll have to help again.*

So he hooted in his superior fashion, "Why, you make one, of course!"

"A grand idea," grunted the soft-eyed doe. "But what shall we use to make the girl a warm winter coat?"

The family of deer put their heads together and tried to think of what they could use to make the coat.

The majestic old stag, who was very brave and often ventured far from the safety of the meadow and the surrounding trees, stomped his feet and grunted, "I have a plan. Just beyond those trees is a fence, and beyond the fence is a field. Twice every day, a farmer brings his sheep to the field to graze. The sheep are now wearing their winter coats, ready for the cold weather that will soon be here. We shall go to the field and ask the sheep if they will each give us a little of their woolly coats so that we can make a warm winter coat for the girl."

"A splendid idea," everyone agreed, and off

they went in search of the sheep pasture.

Dozens of sheep grazed happily in the field.

"We shall ask them kindly if they will share some of their warm woolly coats, so that we can make a winter coat for the girl," grunted the majestic old stag.

When asked, the sheep agreed to each give a little of their wool so that the girl would have a warm coat for the winter.

"The weather has turned cold already. We must hurry to make the coat for the girl," grunted the doe with the soft brown eyes.

"But how do we make the wool into yarn?" asked another doe.

"We shall ask the old squirrel who spun the beautiful silver dress for the girl to show us how to spin the wool into yarn," decided the soft-eyed doe.

So they hurried off to visit the clever old squirrel who had made the dress.

Once they had learned how to spin the wool into yarn, the deer worked as fast as they could. It took them many days to spin enough yarn to make a coat.

"Now what do we do with it?" one of the does asked.

"We must ask the birds who wove the shoes for the girl if they will show us how to weave," grunted the soft-eyed doe.

The birds were happy to help. The deer wove as quickly as they could, but it took

them many more days to complete the coat.

When they had finished weaving, the family of deer looked at their work.

"Oh, what a fine, warm winter coat!" the does grunted softly.

"But it needs just one more thing," said the majestic old stag. "It needs buttons, and I know just what to use."

From out of his antlers he drew a small black ball of something fuzzy. "It is wool from a lonely black sheep we saw in the field," he grunted. "The black sheep will be so proud if we use his wool for the buttons on the coat."

When it was finally completed, the deer family admired the coat.

"All we have to do now is wait for the girl to come back to the meadow to find it," grunted the doe with the soft brown eyes.

The weather was changing quickly. Blustery winds blew through the trees and across the meadow. The once brightly colored leaves had turned old and dry, and the wind lifted them up, dancing and swirling in the air.

"Maybe it will be too cold now for the girl to come," worried the family of deer. They stood silently in the shelter of the pine trees, watching and waiting.

Then, there she was.

The girl walked slowly into the meadow, the dried leaves crunching under her feet. She was wearing the new shoes and the silvery dress that the birds and squirrels had made for her. Over the dress, she wore an old grey shawl to keep out the chill in the air. She looked around, hoping to see her new friends, but none were out today.

As she got closer and closer to the log, she thought she could see something new poking out of the hollow in the log where she found the shoes and the dress. *Yes, there's something there, and I think it's for me!* she thought to herself. It was very white and very woolly. She gently tugged and pulled until she had the mysterious object out of the hollow.

"Oh!" she exclaimed. "What a beautiful, warm winter coat!" She hurriedly took off the shawl and slid her arms into the sleeves of the coat, fastening it with the fuzzy black buttons. *How warm I feel, and how the birds and animals must love me!* she thought.

She then saw the family of deer, who had silently crept up to see how she liked the coat they had made just for her. "The coat is so beautiful, and it will keep me warm all winter long. Thank you, deer family, thank you!" she called to them.

The sky was darkening and black clouds hovered overhead. *I must leave now, before it rains*, thought the girl. *But there is something I must do first.* She very carefully folded the old grey shawl and pushed it into the hollow where her animal friends had left their gifts for her. She hoped that maybe someone who needed it might find it.

Because she knew that it would be many weeks before she would be able to return to the meadow, the girl sat back down on the log for a little while to think. *I am so lucky. I've* made lots of new friends who care about me, and I have comfy new shoes, a beautiful new silvery dress, and a lovely warm winter coat. Why do I still feel so sad?

If only I had...

Winter

The birds and animals of the meadow scurried around, searching for dried grasses, twigs, and leaves to use in their nests, burrows, and dens, so that they would be warm and comfortable in the coming cold weather. Those who would stay in their homes, sleeping away the long winter days, gathered and stored the food they would need. The family of deer found a good stand of pine trees, which would provide a protective canopy from the rain and snow.

Except for the pines, the trees were bare of leaves. Their branches appeared grey and forlorn against the cloudy sky.

Then the rains came: first a gentle drizzle that softened the earth, then a steady downpour that went on day after day, drenching everything from the treetops to the meadow floor and leaving big, muddy puddles everywhere. Just as quickly as the rain started, it stopped, but it was so cold that the puddles froze and icicles hung from tree limbs like ghostly fingers.

Next came clear, bright days, but it was still very cold. The creatures of the meadow woke up every morning to see frost on the ground and nearby bushes. Then came the snow—the trees wore white hats, and a beautiful blanket of fresh white covered the meadow.

Now and then a few animal tracks could be seen, made by the creatures who were brave enough to venture outside. The deer were snug in their warm winter coats, and they often came into the meadow looking for food.

The animals watched from afar as the girl and her granny threw snowballs and built a snowman. The girl always wore the woolly white coat they had made for her. The soft-eyed doe and the majestic old stag smiled knowingly at one another as they watched their own children frolicking in the soft snow. Winter had come and would stay for many weeks.

Daughter of The Wind

The girl had not been to sit on the log by the meadow for a very long time, but on this day the sun was out, the snow had melted, and it was such a lovely early spring day. Yes, she would go to the meadow. It was still a little cool outside, so she wrapped herself in her warm winter coat and set out for the meadow.

The new grass was soft under her feet.

There were buds and new green leaves already growing on the tree branches, and the air smelled fresh and clean. The girl looked around as she approached the log. She was disappointed to find that the old grey shawl was still tucked inside the hollow.

None of her new friends were out and about yet. She wished they were there, because she was beginning to feel sad again. She knew she should be happy because she had so much, but she thought, *If only I had…*

As she sat daydreaming on the log, she heard a huffing and puffing. She looked up and saw an old woman making her way across the meadow. When the old woman reached the girl, she asked, "May I sit with you for a while, child? I've walked a long way today, and my old bones are tired."

The girl scooted aside to make room for the old woman to sit. They sat together in silence until the old woman caught her breath. "I see that you're very sad," the old woman observed. "Why would any child be sad on such a wonderful spring day?"

The girl was quiet for a long time. Then she replied, "I should be happy. I have lots of new friends here in the meadow; the birds made me these shoes, the rabbits let me play with them, the squirrels made me this dress, and the deer made this warm winter coat for me."

"Ah," said the old woman. "Then it must be something even more important. Let's start at the beginning." Settling herself more comfortably on the log, she placed her hand on the girl's knee. "First, we must introduce ourselves. My name is Daisy. What is your name, child?"

With tears in her eyes, the girl told her, "Granny always just calls me 'child.' I have no name." The old woman didn't quite know what to make of that, so she thought for a minute, then asked, "What makes you think that you have no name?"

"Well," began the girl, "a long time ago, Granny wrote some letters on a piece of paper for me, and she said it was my name. I haven't learned to read yet, but I know my ABCs and I can sound out some words." Picking up a stick from the ground, she smoothed the dirt below her feet and wrote "N-O-N-A-M-E" in the soft earth.

"Ah, but you do have a name, don't you see?" said Daisy. "It's just that you have all of the letters jumbled up, and you're missing another E."

She then took the stick from the girl's hand and rearranged the letters to write "A-N-E-M-O-N-E."

"Like mine, your name is the same as a flower that blooms in the springtime. Your flower grows near trees, close to a meadow— just like this one."

"So what is my name?" the girl asked.

"I think you're smart enough to sound it out yourself," Daisy replied, so the girl took the stick and carefully formed the letters into groups. She read out loud, "AN-EM-ON-E."

"Yes, your name is Anemone." Daisy took out an old, well-used book from her pocket. "This book tells us all about the birds, animals, and plants that live in and around this meadow. Inside, we'll find a picture of an anemone so you can see what it looks like and learn about it."

When they finally found the picture in the book, the girl smiled, happy and excited to see that she had been named after such a lovely flower. Meanwhile, Daisy was busy reading more about anemones. "'Often, flower names have another meaning,'" she read out loud. "Another name for 'Anemone' is 'Daughter of the Wind.'"

The girl looked up in wonder. "I have a name!" she cried. "I am Anemone, Daughter of the Wind."

Meanwhile, unnoticed by the old woman and the girl, many eyes and ears were watching and listening to what was happening. Birds twittered amongst themselves, "She has a name, she has a name!" Rabbits, squirrels, and deer whispered to each other, "That's what she wanted most—her very own name."

The girl rose from the log. She looked around and saw all of her friends from the meadow. "Thank you for caring so much about me," she said. "Thank you birds, for the new shoes; thank you rabbits, for letting me play with you; thank you squirrels, for the beautiful silvery dress; thank you deer, for the warm winter coat; and thank you owl, for being so wise!"

What joy she felt as she stepped into the meadow. "I have a name, a beautiful name!" She started to run, the ribbon in her hair streaming behind like a silky red flag.

The next thing she knew, all of the birds

and animals of the meadow were following her. Even the wise old owl flew up high with the birds. The rabbits hopped along close to her heels with the squirrels hurrying behind, trying to keep up. Last came the family of deer, led by the majestic old stag and the soft-eyed doe.

As the girl and her creature friends ran and frolicked throughout the meadow, no longer sad and unhappy, the girl shouted out for all the world to hear: "I have a name—I am Anemone, Daughter of the Wind!"

Exhausted, Anemone came to a stop. Suddenly, she remembered that Daisy must still be waiting at the edge of the meadow.

I must go and thank her, she thought to herself.

She looked over toward the log where

Daisy had been sitting. There was no sign of the old woman. She had disappeared, and so had the old grey shawl.

"Thank you, Miss Daisy," Anemone whispered, as she happily skipped across the meadow to where the old white house and her granny waited.

About the Author

Born and raised in England, the author is a great grandmother who has loved to read since she was very young. She believes that a child's imagination is a wonderful thing, and that books are a great way to foster that imagination.

Like all parents and grandparents, she's read many bedtime stories, but the ones the children enjoyed best were the stories she created from her own imagination. Late in life, she started to write her thoughts down and *If Only I Had* ... is the result. Enjoy!